Bucking Horse

HETTY BURLINGAME BEATTY

1957

HOUGHTON MIFFLIN COMPANY BOSTON • THE RIVERSIDE PRESS CAMBRIDGE

To

ELSIE and PALEY RAK

and specially for

CHUCKIE

Wild One was born among the scrub oak at the far-
thest end of the ranch. All Summer he ran wild in the
hills with his mother and the other horses and colts.

They called him Wild One because he ran so fast the cowboys couldn't catch him to brand him. He was afraid of their loud shouts and swinging ropes, and when he heard them galloping over the hills he ran as fast as he could and hid among the scrub oak.

When Fall came, the cowboys rounded up all the horses and colts in the hills and herded them down to the big pasture near the ranch house. Wild One ran with them but he kept just as far ahead of the cowboys as he could.

When they reached the pasture, Danny, the rancher's son, came out to see the new colts.

Wild One was standing near the fence, still frightened and panting from the long run. As soon as he saw Danny, he snorted through his nose and was all ready to run again. But Danny just sat on the fence and talked softly to him. He didn't shout and swing a rope the way the cowboys did, so Wild One wasn't afraid.

All that Winter Danny came often to the pasture to see Wild One. He talked gently to him and brought him apples and carrots to eat, and Wild One soon grew to love and trust him.

When Spring came the cowboys finally cornered Wild One in the pasture. They roped him and branded him with the ranch brand, so they would always know to whom he belonged. After that, Wild One was more afraid of the cowboys than before, and when they turned him loose in the hills for the Summer he was wilder than ever.

The cowboys seldom saw him at all because he ran so fast. And the bigger he grew the wilder he got and the faster he ran.

The next Fall when the horses and colts were herded back to the pasture for the Winter, Danny came out to greet Wild One with his pockets full of apples and carrots. Wild One nickered and ate them happily. That Winter Danny and Wild One became better friends than ever and Danny could do anything with him.

As soon as Wild One was full grown, the cowboys said it was time to ride him. They herded him into the corral and threw a rope around his neck so he couldn't run. Then they put a saddle on his back and a hackamore on his nose.

Wild One was terrified but the rope choked him when he tried to run. Danny sat on the fence watching. Al-

though he hated to see Wild One so frightened, he knew this was the way the cowboys trained all the colts.

The cowboys were mighty good riders so they were sure they could ride Wild One.

When Wild One was all saddled, Joe and Cliff held him while Jake climbed into the saddle. Then they took off the rope and let him go.

Wild One leaped into the air and began to buck as hard as he could. He bucked and twisted and bucked

some more, and he threw Jake
right over the corral fence!

Then Joe tried to ride him. Jake and Cliff held him while Joe got on. But as soon as they let him go, Wild One leaped into the air and bucked harder than ever.

He twisted and bucked and jumped, and he threw Joe right over the corral gate!

Next Cliff tried to ride him. Cliff had won prizes riding in the rodeo, so he was sure he could ride Wild One.

As soon as Cliff got on, Wild One bucked harder than he had ever bucked before. He jumped and twisted and bucked with all his might, but he couldn't throw Cliff

off, no matter how hard he tried. So Wild One
just reared over backward and rolled
Cliff in the dirt instead!

When Wild One had thrown off all the cowboys, he walked over to Danny and reached his nose out to be patted.

"Maybe I could ride him," Danny said. "He likes me and he doesn't seem to like you fellows at all."

"Go ahead and try," laughed the cowboys. "We'll pick up the pieces if we can find them!"

So Danny climbed onto Wild One's back. Wild One just tossed his head and walked around the corral as if he'd been ridden all his life. After all, Danny was his friend and Wild One wasn't afraid.

"I'll be hanged!" Cliff shouted. "That horse throws us all over the place, and the kid rides him as if he were a tame old plug!"

After that Danny rode Wild One all the time. He helped the cowboys herd the cattle in the hills.

Wild One was smart and he soon learned how to herd cattle. The cowboys had to admit he was a good cow-pony, even if they couldn't handle him.

Whenever an unruly cow or a weaner

calf broke out of the herd, Danny and Wild One went after it. They always brought it back because Wild One could run so fast.

One morning when Danny and the cowboys were saddling their horses in the corral, the cowboys asked Danny if they could try riding Wild One again.

"Go ahead and try," Danny said. "I don't mind if Wild One doesn't."

So Jake tried . . .

Then   Joe tried . . .

And then Cliff tried. . . .

25

The cowboys were angrier and more ashamed than ever! Then Jake had an idea. "Let's take Wild One to the rodeo and see if the champion riders can ride him."

Cliff and Joe thought it was a wonderful idea, and Danny thought it would be fun to find out, too.

They loaded Wild One on the ranch truck and started off to the rodeo. The cowboys rode on the front seat, and Danny rode in back with Wild One so he wouldn't be frightened and try to jump out of the truck.

When they got there they led Wild One over to the rodeo judge. The cowboys told him that none of them could ride him and that they wanted to see if the champion riders could. The judge knew what a wonderful rider Cliff was, so he looked Wild One over.

"He doesn't look very wild," the judge said. "But if he's as wild as you say he's just what we need for the champions to ride for the prize money. They're the three best riders in the country and it takes a really tough horse to throw them!"

First of all the County Champion tried. He got on Wild One in the saddling chute. As soon as the gate was opened Wild One came out bucking as if he'd swallowed a stick of dynamite.

He bucked and twisted and bucked, and in no time at all he threw the County Champion right into the middle of the audience!

Then the State Champion tried. Wild One bucked and twisted and jumped harder than ever, and in next to no time he threw the State Champion right into the middle of the brass band!

Then the National Champion tried. He was the best rider in the whole country, so everyone was sure he could ride Wild One.

Wild One bucked and twisted and jumped and bucked some more. He bucked so hard he nearly

turned inside out, but he couldn't throw the National Champion off. So he reared over backward and rolled him in the dirt instead!

The crowd shouted with laughter and the Champion was very angry. His beautiful silk shirt was ruined and his pride was in even worse shape!

Wild One stood still in the middle of the arena wondering what next. Danny thought the show was all over and he decided to ride Wild One back to the truck.

He walked across the arena to Wild One and climbed up into the saddle. Wild One just walked off quietly toward the truck!

To Danny's amazement, the crowd began to cheer wildly. They stood up on the seats and threw their hats in the air and cheered and cheered.

Then the rodeo judge ran out of the judge's stand with a big silver cup in one hand and the prize money in the other. He handed them both to Danny!

After all Danny was the only one who could ride Wild One!